THE DEVONIAN COMEDY

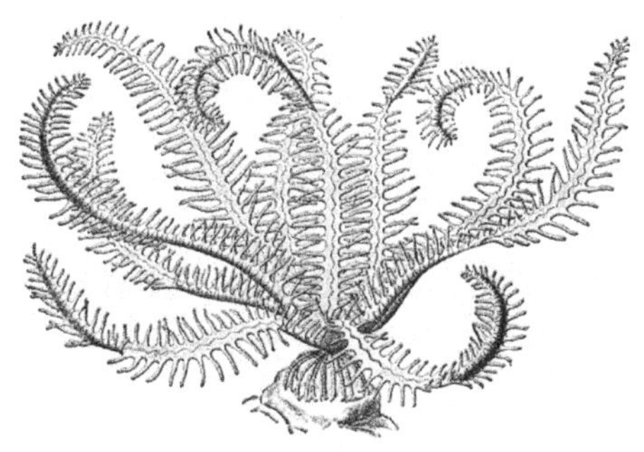

A TRILOBITE TRILOGY

by

DON T. ALIGHIERI

Sastra Books
415 W. Delaware St.
Decatur, MI 49045

ISBN# 9798671197556

Cover and other art cobbled from the public domain. Quotations from Dante's *The Divine Comedy,* the Henry Wadsworth Longfellow translation.

For E. D.

In Memoriam

There may be an Orpheus who follows yet
Footprints his Eurydice left . . . .

CONTENTS

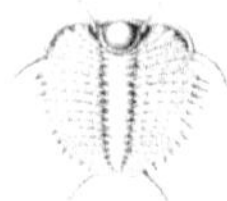

TO THE READER......6

PROLOGUE......11

PARADISO......22

PURGATORIO......58

INFERNO......69

LIMBO......83

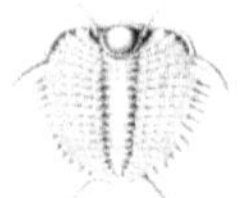

Shells and divine consciousness adhere to each other, as light permeates matter and glows through it.

The body is glowing shells.

Isaac Luria

TO THE READER

The Devonian Comedy was not the book I foresaw going into print when I set my first manuscript on the chief editor's desk at Sastra Books. The untitled original was my translation of the Lobster Archives which in large part contained a history of the trilobites, their culture and their civilization, preserved by the lobsters who translated it into their own language, which in turn I had rendered into English, "un-mothering" myself from my mother tongue, while learning the best I could of theirs over a period of several years.

But I could not have recast the trilobite material unless I received it first unrefined but whole from the lobsters; what is more, I would have received nothing from the lobsters unless the crayfish had not approached the lobsters with a word or a "snap of their pincers" (so to speak) on my behalf. I have long had antiquarian interests, and hearing of an ancient legacy still extant among another species excited me as much as fossil microbes on Mars would excite a biologist of the extraterrestrial.

You, reader, may be one of those who would think that discovering such fossil microbes more probable than conversing with either lobsters or crayfish, much less learning from them of a vanished arthropod civilization. You would be one of those who consider the "Doolittle Syndrome," to which I succumbed several years ago, at the very least a maiming delusion, if not a feigned illness to attract sympathy and money from a gullible public.

Here is not the place to persuade you otherwise, but sufficient evidence has come to the fore to consider the syndrome a feature of contemporary life. My crayfish friends maintain that it is a result of “digital excesses and planetary stresses” of human origin which have forced the human body to crouch in *techno-isolation* for excessively prolonged periods of time. What is owed to either the natural order or the cultural has become greatly confused, to the detriment of human kind. Folks who have become so isolated may begin to seek unmediated contact with the mineral, plant, animal, and even celestial kingdoms. This contact remains a birthright which society neglects. In counterpoint to this, animal species threatened by extinction have abandoned their traditional modes of communication which had long formed a boundary between themselves and humanity, in a desperate attempt to communicate directly their plight and hopes for survival.

The reader may be familiar with what is called “hive collapse” decimating the pollinator honey bees. A “hidden” and contributing factor to hive collapse is the exhaustion bees suffer in attempting to reach and inform the human race of the havoc of climate change. Bees “dance” to show their cohorts the way to the nearest dandelion or clover patch. Enlivened by an inspiration altogether not unworthy, they thought they could learn “to dance” the Roman alphabet, and thus translate their thoughts into the many human languages which used such a script.

This was an effort undertaken with great devotion, yet doomed, for the bees had chosen a hand-written script of the alphabet now no longer taught at the primary level, so that no matter how exquisite the form, the content was lost to humans who came across it, having themselves never set pen to paper from childhood. Whole bee hives went aloft following their queens to "sky-write" against buffeting winds and spumes of pollution, only to perish from their exertions. A victim of Doolittle Syndrome meandering on a beach strewn with exhausted bees, parsed their feeble gestures, and reported later to doctors before expiring: *"What the bees have writ, only I have read. We're better off dead."*

Of digital excesses, initially I suffered only the common complaints: eye-strain, headaches, the gradual suppression of breath, approaching almost almost imperceptibly, as does a cockroach horde in the dark. Hours may be spent in such a state. When the moment comes to raise body to standing, one's organism seems ill-suited to navigate in three-dimensional space—as if it had become a diplocodus thrown and beached on a shore, without surrounding water to displace weight, granting it freedom of movement.

If such conditions persist, and are accompanied as in my case with severe migraines, the Doolittle Syndrome may precipitate. My physician predicted this outcome after I had formed a passionate longing for natural light, and that of the most exotic kind, beyond that of the sun and moon, which could not take me far enough from the glaring screens of digital devices. The flickering delights of the Great Bear and the Pleiades were for my eyes to drink in, wines of a vintage measured in light-years.

My wife and I, seated before my physician hand in

hand, initially took comfort in his opinion that once the complete syndrome had set in, I could still lead a "productive and happy" life, that phrase an epitaph common enough which many wish to be etched on their gravestones. We had already learned of "DLS" victims who had turned the aberration into profit through music, with or without accompanying YouTube videos, exploiting the public's love for cute animals and fetching melodies: *Songs of the Hump-backed Whales (Now Translated into English for the First Time), Kangaroo Carols, The Elephant Elegies,* and *Koala Komic Monologues,* were only a few of the albums in our collection that had ensured a steady income stream for their creators.

But which creature's language I would suddenly find myself receptive to was a matter of chance. As my wife had wished for a rare order of beauty in the species: a polar bear, a snow leopard, a white rhino; we voyaged to climes favorable to their kind, expecting a spontaneous communication to arise. It was her despair, when back home and traversing a small creek hidden behind a small grove of sumac in the back of a fast-food restaurant, that I picked up the coo and clatter of a gaggle of ordinary crayfish, whose songs and melodies were dull, lyrics uninspired, and coarse jokes unappealing to human kind. They had, however, access to records of the long history of the arthropods, which I began to record and transcribe on many legal pads, in addition to becoming fluent in their language.

The path of marriage soon became so wide between my wife and I that neither of us could reach across it. I once caught part of a phone conversation between her and a friend. “He spends his time crouched on all fours, listening to his 'friends'—those dull brown critters. Sickly white underneath when you turn them over. Well, yes. Right. That may be what *he* is like, too. Haven't seen that side of him for some time, if you know what I mean.”

We did part, as amicably as we could. I recently received a photograph of her with her husband and their girl, a child of ten, raised in the best of “hydroponic” environments available. It is a testament to the powers of ignorance and innocence that a child can look upon either the Milky Way or a lit-up shopping mall with the same moon-eyed wonder, and I am sure the child had seen plenty of the latter and little of the former except through photography or film, of course made by somebody else. Meanwhile, I had plowed on with my translation of the Lobster Archives.

The editor at Sastra Books, assuming that I had created the language and history of an imagined culture, mistakenly thought my translation a magnificent fiction, worthy of publication, but *only* as such. He even thought I was continuing the ruse when I maintained that I had translated a history based on a species' written records; that these records, scattered in oceans throughout the world, were temporarily placed in my hands by their custodians the lobsters, who would consider it a great affront if humans did not recognize the veracity and merit of the records or appreciate the generosity of the lobsters in sharing the fate of the trilobites, which they opined foreshadowed much of the fate of human kind.

The editor furthered his case, remarking that if published

as historical fact, the archives would only appeal to a small but enthusiastic audience, akin to those who passionately pursue such notions as the "seeding" of Earth by aliens from other planets, or the "hollow" Earth harboring civilizations hitherto unknown to we surface dwellers. The message of the archives, if there were one, would be lost to the greater public, unless the appetite for conspiracy theories or "junk thought" swelled as large as that for "junk food."

I did, and still do, see his point. At the same time, I could not produce physical evidence of the Lobster Archives, as those were conserved by the lobster elders, and in no way could be copied or removed from their tabernacles of learning scattered in underwater caves throughout the world.

I had pleaded with my lobster liaisons that the saga of the trilobites, their emergence, rise and decline, so pertinent to our times of climate and cultural upheaval, would not reach print unless some in their community were willing to step forth on the public stage and make an appeal for recognition of their ancestors. Sastra Books would arrange speaking engagements, talk show interviews, produce websites and blogs, set up Twitter or Facebook accounts and so forth at no little cost in time and effort to itself, if at least a lobster or two would show up and bear witness to historical truth.

One crustacean colleague, who would often speak for the many, remarked: "What good would that do? If the majority of you humans do not consider the well-wrought opinions of your best and brightest on cultural decline or climate change, I cannot see why you should listen to us except for the mere novelty of seeing critters, such as we, bloviate, sticking our heads out of the tank at a sea food restaurant, or rising up from your dinner plate to deliver a silver-tongued harangue against your own kind. Only the novelty of our appearance would fetch you, until you tired of it, eager for the next distraction, this desire an epidemic side-effect of the pursuit of comfort, convenience and consumption."

Here the lobster scuttled backwards a bit to pause, then continued: "In a way though, you are very much like we lobsters. As the planet heats up, you will squirm and rattle a bit as we do in the boiling pot. And then, for many of you, all will be silent. The hope is that some with mettle will survive. How can you enter the cauldron of rebirth, with cell phone in hand, and expect to tread its turbulent waters?" He then begged to depart as he volunteered ministering to those suffering from the "Triple S," or "Soft Shell Syndrome" a plague issuing from the over-heated global seas.

I could only hope to publish anything of the trilobite saga if I recast it in the mold of *poesy* instead of historiography. I thought a blend of Darwin and Dante would do, my own name a near rhyme to that of the Italian Master. While I respect Dante, I have reversed the path of the poet: my narrative goes from Paradise, through Purgatory to Hell, ending with a small coda in Limbo. I have rendered the "inferno" of the trilobites a chilly place. Not only is this in accord with Dante's description of the utmost depths of Hades, but also echoes the theory that the trilobites died off during a period of global cooling. An immense growth of plant life increased the oxygen supply, which did not trap sunlight. The trilobites went down with the dip in temperature.

May what my whimsy
Spins from borrowed things,
Charm you.

Don T. Alighieri

* * *

PROLOGUE

In a period of Earth remote from the birth of time, which arose unencumbered by numbers, even after billions of years, the land remained silent, evolution itself being little evolved. Volcanic eruptions, earthquakes, great winds and thunderstorms were unheard and unseen; there were no organisms with organs to sense these ambient vibrations, except for those in the seas which harbored life long before the tumult and tenderness of its pageantry would creep beyond the waters. Water afforded organisms a lush efflorescence, from which emerged the trilobites, one of the most successful species that the planet has known, establishing a good portion of the genome for the crabs, lobsters and crayfish with whom we share the planet today, although the trilobites themselves are extinct.

Being a success from an evolutionary perspective does not mean one "retires early." Rather it means evolution confers a longevity to the either the individual or the group, as the creature's features are compatible with its environment and its stresses. While not particularly beautiful in form, the trilobite body exhibited a pronounced symmetry, Nature having discovered this a valuable attribute for the multi-cellular and motile. And while the trilobite exoskeleton was no doubt somewhat ungainly and clunky, it proved an effective barrier against predators. Trilobites exemplified that the "race not always goes to the swiftest," except perhaps in matters of reproduction, wherein the fossil record indicates they enjoyed a pronounced fecundity, perhaps outstripping and exhausting the efforts of natural enemies to replenish their own kind. As trilobites scavenged remains raining down endlessly upon the ocean floor, they proved invaluable to the health of the ecosystem, a "pool of labor" which Nature could not do without for eons, and generously multiplied their kind. The different species of trilobites are estimated in the thousands.

Although in some ways hardly comparable, the trilobite and the dinosaur were both, in separate epochs, the crowning achievements of evolution. Summoned into existence by forces larger than themselves, so did they succumb to the same forces in their demise, some returned to dust, some fossilized, the molecules of others sank into a primordial biomass, emerging later as a drop of gas through a technology highly adapted to the human habits of consumption and thoughtless dependence.

Trilobites might be better displayed to advantage in an animated film, of the kind usually released during the winter holidays or the summertime, produced with children in mind, but with enough wit and humor to amuse accompanying parents or chaperon. Consider the saga of a young girl trilobite turned detective:

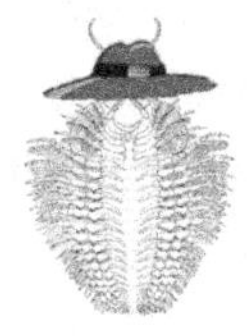

YOU'LL THRILL MEETING TRILL!
SHE'S A PRIVATE EYE WITH TWENTY FEET AND THE SEA BED IS HER BEAT. SCUTTLING SOON TO A THEATER NEAR YOU!
Rated PG for audiences gone post-*Genesis*

Budget allowing for what are called high "production values," a well-known composer could furnish a score including a song worthy of an Oscar nomination—a personal anthem, lyrics simple but fetching, perhaps expressing sentiments of hope and renewal in the face of personal struggle or failure. It would have, in the year following its release, innumerable cover versions done by various artists, becoming not only a favorite of marching bands, but found in the hymnals of megachurches. Re-arranged for a string ensemble, a figure skating pair would scar the ice with arabesques, following the tune towards an Olympic gold medal. Originally entitled "*The Molting Song from Trill,*" it would become more commonly known by the first line of its chorus:

Cast off your shell—
It's old, not like you;
Look to the sun,
Let's begin anew,
Listen dear crustacea,
Every day's a birthday, yeah,
Cast off your shell!

Had Nature forestalled playing her trump card of

extinction, the destinies of trilobites and humans may have interwoven in many ways, ensuring the arthropod a more honored place not only in natural history, but in our cultures and civilizations.

Known as the "sparrow of the waters" to native North American tribes, these peoples were not the first to recognize the trilobites as an indispensable source of food. The slaves of ancient Egypt could not have built the cities and monuments of their pharaohs without the trilobites of the upper and lower Nile and its delta. Although royal families and the priestly caste refrained from ingesting such plebeian fare, even the smallest village had a temple to honor the trilobite god whom the pharaoh would deign to honor in a special three-day festival held once a year: the monarch would take one ceremonial bite of a trilobite baked on coals, to the roar of public approval and adulation. A minority of historians, much like those who believe Francis Bacon wrote the plays of Shakespeare, contend that the trilobite divinity played a greater role in the spiritual lives of the Egyptians, and that the pharaoh's head dress was modeled on the skull of the trilobite. The following "reconstruction" is highly suggestive of this transformation.

Babylonian astrologers assigned a trilobite to that constellation we now call Scorpio, a reversal of ancient convention that they would call sacrilegious. Although sharing many characteristics, the trilobite denoted a benign aspect, while the scorpion, an adverse one. During times of turmoil, scandal, or anarchy, a popular proverb ran, "There's a scorpion among the trilobites." The trilobites also found their way into the diet of the Romans, who crushed the shells into a powder which enhanced the binding powers of their remarkable cement, microscopic analysis of which reveals trilobite particles from species found from within the Mediterranean, and as far from the city of Rome as the rivers Thames and Danube.

In the early years of the Christian era, "apocryphal" gospels later deemed heretical have Christ asking his disciples to "Consider the trilobites of the shores" instead of "the lilies of the field." The sects which favored this version argued that "trilobites" were more logical for "fishers of men" to consider than flower blossoms never found at the seaside. It is true historically that the fishermen on the Sea of Galilee set trilobite traps, hoping to pick up a drachma or two, supplementing income gained from the sale of perch and trout. A more Gnostic interpretation expounded that the living trilobite flesh, tender and vibrant, is encased in a hard shell, just as the soul inhabits a dense body. They also claimed that the horizontal head resembled the horizontal beam of the cross upon which Christ died, and that the ends of this beam turned downwards, signifying the burdens and pains of earthly consciousness which Christ had to bear. The trilobite sect of Christianity flourished in the third century, especially in the hermit cave dwellings of the desert saints in Egypt.

Some Biblical scholars claim that the drawings of trilobites in these caves have nothing at all to do with Christianity, but are simply a late pagan resurgence of worship of the god of the trilobites. However, the discovery of a group in Ethiopia, whose major art work includes a gold cross with a trilobite crucified thereon, has revived again debate among archaeologists. The latest hot item from the "New Age" paraphernalia industry is a trilobite bracelet charm which comes wrapped in parchment describing its history and use for attracting "positive" energies, the same, supposedly, that kept the Desert Fathers optimistic, goal-oriented and motivated two thousand years ago. Recall Saint Anthony, whose charm, the parchment describes, had slipped off his wrist into the sand, a breach in his aura that let in a flood of morbid temptations for days on end.

In the early Nineteenth Century, during the Napoleonic campaign in Egypt, not only did French archaeologists unearth the Rosetta Stone, but the Emperor too made a discovery which again linked trilobites with inspiring head-dress. Parisian bakers celebrated the victory in Egypt with *croissants* in the shape of trilobites, and jewelers cast gold and silver ear rings in similar molds.

"Hey, Bro!" **!?**

Throughout the Twentieth Century and well into recent times, the trilobites continued to survive in healthy numbers, but only as a food source for those in developing nations. Industrialized countries bred them on large farms to be used in fertilizing major grain crops. Sometimes viewed as a nuisance, trilobites often fell victim to developers who would bull-doze them out of beach fronts. Environmentalists and animal rights activists hardly complained or raised a cry, for it seemed there was always more than an ample supply of the arthropods, and truth was, stepping barefoot on small ones often spoiled a good run and splash on the sea side.

It seemed as if science had exhausted all that could be known about the trilobites, and the economy had extracted all it could be gotten out of them except amusement. There was hardly a child in the developing world who did not have at one time a "trillarium," the trilobite having replaced the goldfish as a "first pet." As with the goldfish, the trilobite either outgrew its dwelling if taken well care of, or floated belly up if not. Alive and large, more difficult to give away or release in the wild; if dead even more of a problem to flush down the toilet. A fad that would have its cycles of resurgence like the yoyos, trillariums date from the nineteen twenties onward, some versions fetching good prices as collectibles. The Depression Era *art deco* versions are favored finds at flea markets and antique stalls.

In the beginning of the current century the phrase "canary in a coal mine" was rapidly replaced with "trilobite on a shoreline," for rising global temperatures spawned several types of fungal infections that devastated populations of trilobites world-wide. Attempts to breed disease resistant strains met with mixed results, while a hitherto unknown and "blind" species was found inhabiting the depths of the Mariana Trenches; biochemical analysis revealed that an extract from its *medulla oblongata* was extraordinarily effective in arresting the progress of dementia. More attention was now paid to the trilobite than ever before; it became a symbol of both the fear of climactic apocalypse and the hope of a suffering eliminated or assuaged.

In this "alternative history," there is as little fact, just as there is little of Dante in the following "*Devonian Comedy.*" Those who prefer their history or poetry unadulterated might best lay this narrative aside. Others may not find such reading an idle exercise. To paraphrase that rhyme printed on the side rear-view mirrors of our vehicles:

Species from the past
Seen in the mirror,
Are much closer
Than they appear

* * *

PARADISO

Here do the higher creatures
See the footprints of Eternal Power,
Hence they do move onward with ports
Diverse o'er the great sea of being.
Dante

A wide cove on the the Devonian sea, morning waters ruffled by a light warm breeze: the territory of a trilobite tribe who called themselves the "Golden Ones," because (and only because) that was their color, just as there were the Silver Ones, the Speckled, the Bronze, and furthest from them all, the relatively smaller and duskier but cheeky ones known as the "Pygmies." Originally the colors only distinguished one tribe from another, denoting no superiority or inferiority of intelligence or moral character. Although the Golden enjoyed a certain edge in cultural achievements, they saw these only as a surplus, a largess to share with all members of the species, thereby imitating Nature, which had endowed the Golden with so much skill in exploiting a bountiful seabed. There would be almost countless epochs, not all of them happy, in the saga of the Golden Ones, but this earliest was, and would hence be known as the Era of Good Feeling, in which all arthropods, even those unknown to the Golden, could enjoy, so to speak, "a good fling."

Great Senior, the wisest of all the Golden Ones, declared that a "Great Convocation" should be held of all trilobites, at which they could be taught the art of making *trilograms* —messages written by pebbles set in certain patterns invented by Great Senior himself. They could also learn the script of Seaweed-Weaving, a more complicated writing form created by his wife Penelope. There were also the sports of Wave Surfing (again invented by Great Senior as child, with friend Toby), and Toppling, developed by his daughter, Rhonda, and Great Senior's *aide de camp*, Longinus. Toppling involved trilobites climbing on top of one another to reach the highest point possible, sometimes the surface of the sea, often with random and unpredictable currents that challenged the integrity and strength of the column.

The convocation was such a novelty that Penelope thought it could only come about if it coincided with the period of molting and mating, following a groove well-established by Nature to which the species instinctively conformed. This, and given the predilection for trilobites to gather and follow "the group," would ensure a large number at the gathering, itself almost purely "cultural" in essence, and not likely to attract many, at least the first time around. Great Senior a year in advance sent out emissaries all along the coast to contact all trilobite communities both known and unknown, tempting them to attend the Great Convocation by offering baskets of a succulent seaweed cultivated by Penelope.

On a morning only several days away from the event, Great Senior woke from his slumber to the noise of scraping and clambering coming from the top of the ledge underneath which he, his wife, and daughter Rhonda made their home. Trilobites were arriving from all areas of the Devonian waters.

"Do you hear that? Do you hear that?" he shouted, too animated to notice that his wife was not beside him and his daughter was not bustling about in the kitchen preparing breakfast. Penelope was tending her garden, and Rhonda gathering seaweed for the masses that would dine tomorrow. Great Senior smiled as he heard the scraping. No sound, except perhaps the cries of his daughter at birth, had so moved him. He rose up and ran to stick his head out from under the ledge. So thick was the press of legs and shells moving that few if any of the arriving trilobites had noticed the grizzled elder smiling at their passing by.

Great Senior lurched when something fell from above bumping his head, landing in front of him. It was a trilobite child, but of a tribe he had not seen before. The shell was of a pale blue with white streaks in irregular patterns covering the face. Great Senior bent forward and spoke in a tender voice, "Hail to thee, friend! 'Tis a trilobite world!" The little boy shivered with fear, but was able to turn himself upright. A larger one of the same hue, his mother perhaps, leaned from the ledge and swooped him up, giving Great Senior only a backward glance as she scuttled off. The little boy, thought Great Senior, did not speak the language of the Golden. His tribe may not have had much of a language at all.

Great Senior grabbed a drifting strand of seaweed and tied it to the knee joint of the second leg on his right side: a mnemonic device so he might remember to ask one of his emissaries about the habits and customs of that pale tribe.

Mnemonic strategies were also an invention of Great Senior. The right side of the body was devoted to remembering aspects of public projects such as the convocation, while the left was devoted to matters family and private. He had expanded the system to include reminders coded by different colors of seaweed, but this had overburdened the method to such a degree that it often worked against itself, agitating and confusing Great Senior. But this was, after all, a most busy period for himself and all the Golden. With multiple strands trailing from joints of all legs, a prehistoric Merlin so be-cloaked, Great Senior ambled at slow pace, nodding at the trilobites who scuttled by, "Hail to thee!...Hail to thee!...Hail to thee!" He was on his way to see how the amphitheater was filling up, not without tripping on strands he dragged behind him.

II

A mural etched on the side of a massive cliff, much earlier brought underwater by an earthquake, depicted what came to be known as the "standard account" of the Great Convocation. That account had already been written in condensed trilogram or longer seaweed script versions for hundreds of trilobite generations, but the mural could convey the event to the illiterate as well. In the center of the mural stood the dominant figure of the Great Senior, scattering pebbles to the masses in front of him who were gathering in groups to learn the art of making trilograms. On Great Senior's left—Penelope, who unrolled a long stretch of seaweed script which admiring trilobites began to read. On Great Senior's right—Rhonda, his daughter, lovingly gazing at her fiance Longinus, who was teaching younger trilobites how to climb on top of one another.

"A magnificent work of art lost," claimed one pygmy when reports came of the mural's collapse during a second earthquake, generations after it was finished, "but not a loss of history, as there was very little true history in it." A skeptical attitude was typical of the Pygmy Tribe. Pygmies did attend the Great Convocation but they were not represented in the mural. Those attending returned with no arts or skills, explaining to their fellow tribes-folk, "He who pretended to teach, learned the least of all. But he who learned the most, taught us all." The former referred to Great Senior; the latter, to Toby.

III

Penelope stretched in the canopied seaweed hammock at the very center of a small "Sargasso Sea" she had cultivated herself over the years. It was an aquatic garden containing many sorts of seaweeds collected from all shores of the Devonian waters: some weeds for fodder, some for medicine, and others for aphrodisiacs. Although males could visit, this was her domain, a gathering place for the female Golden. It was called the "She-Weedery." Penelope had heard the scraping of the arriving hordes long before her husband did, and sped to the garden for some peace and quiet. Rhonda, her daughter, also awoke, and followed her. Rhonda was now at a far end of the Sargasso with her companions, harvesting the best crop to feed the thousands of convocation attendees.

When she first arrived at the garden, Penelope found a seaweed scroll awaiting her from Longinus, whom Great Senior had sent with assistants to the edge of Golden Community to escort Toby to the convocation. Longinus had already been gone more than a week, and while Great Senior's mind was cluttered with too many convocation details to take notice of his absence, Penelope had begun to wonder if something had gone awry. She was relieved to find the scroll, for this meant that Longinus was at least "all right" enough to report back, no matter what the condition of Toby might be.

Longinus wrote: *Toby irregular, erratic. Sentinels' claws, legs, snapped, broken. Convocation uncertain.*

Why had Longinus sent this to her instead of Great Senior? Most probably because he knew she would be sure to tell her husband. Great Senior would have received it, read it, and forgotten it a second later. But she wondered whether she should tell Great Senior or not. It did not seem that Longinus would arrive in time with Toby. Given her husband's state of mind, that might not make any difference. Great Senior had thought to bring Toby to the convocation in one of his unpredictable instant inspirations, in spite of Penelope's and Rhonda's objections that he had not seen Toby for years, that they hardly had accommodations for him, that Toby might upset domestic as well as greater public arrangements, the least problem being his relatively gargantuan size. Great Senior only recalled the smaller, the "lesser" Toby, not the "greater" one that grew after what became to be called "the accident." Over family objections, he dispatched Longinus with a cohort of sentinels to fetch Toby.

This news from Longinus, thought Penelope, would sadden her daughter, who expected her betrothed for the convocation. Although both daughter and mother were more "culturally" advanced than their neighbors, they, no less than the untutored, were born with ancient and atavistic longings which separation would only sorely aggravate.

IV

If Great Senior had granted Penelope more freedom than other trilobite females, both husband and wife had granted even more to their daughter, Rhonda, who was perhaps the most "agglutinated" male or female of all the trilobites. The common trilobite lived in a state of collective consciousness with other trilobites, meaning that any one trilobite was not conscious of the springs of his or her behavior. Clustered in groups, if two slid down a ledge, collective consciousness meant the others would follow instinctively just to keep the group intact. To agglutinate meant to take a step back from the collective impulse, to pause and consider, and perhaps come up with a new and beneficial pattern. Great Senior and his childhood friend Toby, like many other young trilobites, thought it was great fun when waves would push them around close to shore, provided of course that they didn't get too close and pushed out of the water. But this was a random enjoyment. Either the wave carried you or not. Great Senior and Toby agglutinated the phenomenon: took turns studying the waves, when and how they carried them, and what body position to assume when the "right wave" came. Thus wave surfing came into being. Riding a wave was no longer an infrequent thrill—but now an art with predictable and satisfying outcomes.

Rhonda had already mated and bore a child in an earlier, collectivist phase of her development. This was the "traditional" trilobite way. Trilobites cared for one another, and offspring would move from clan to clan; there was no fear of losing a child or of a child being abandoned. The bias of the mass was towards safety and social cohesion. Rhonda would occasionally see her child, having only minimal motherly contact with the boy. But there was no danger of him floundering without nurture. The emotional strength of this contact would vary with the prevailing consciousness—individual or collective, just as the reception of old fashioned radio signals varied with atmospheric conditions, but it would always be there.

Those who were close to Great Senior and to Penelope had been initiated (or sometimes initiating themselves), into agglutination. This was true of Longinus and Rhonda, who more or less anticipated becoming a couple like her parents —another pair who would do much for their species. It was a hallmark notion of those who had passed through the ceremony of agglutination that "things would always get better."

Yet this agglutination had its drawbacks, especially when, as now, Longinus was gone on a special mission. Without him, Rhonda felt like a "stranger in a strange land," and no other trilobite could replace his individual self for her. So few of them had any individual selves anyhow.

Her father angered her with his imperative that Toby attend the convocation. She understood that they were friends, but Toby, she thought, would hardly understand what was going on, however much sentiment might demand he be present. She remembered her father taking her to see him when she was a young girl. For Toby's own safety and that of others, Great Senior had him corralled in a wide depression, sentinels standing guard who brought him food, or let him walk about on a leash made of tightly bound seaweed. Toby was at least three or four times larger than the largest trilobite she had seen at home. He had a huge scar running across the top of his head down towards his face. The scar, her father said, came from "the accident," which had also triggered a glandular imbalance, leading to his monstrous growth. One obsidian eye was dull with scar tissue while the other appeared bright and normal.

When she first met Toby, Rhonda saw her father and Toby grab one another's fore claws and shed tears. They were true friends. Toby's good eye brightened even more when Great Senior introduced Rhonda. He, however, quickly relapsed, staying there for minutes, sometimes waking up and uttering nonsense in words often unknown, and then slumbering again. As if in a trance, he journeyed to a world not his own. On the occasion of their visit, Toby aroused from a short snooze with the following:

Five fathom deep
Thy brothers and sisters lie
Shall we go there
You and I?

Toby fully awoke some hours later, then seeming quite normal, enjoying his repast with Great Senior and Rhonda. When her father was saying his farewell, Toby only said:

Is it a male hint,
Or a female hint?
Maybe its two, two,
Two hints in one.
Tell me next time;
O, What fun!

Great Senior turned away in sadness and shook his head. Rhonda climbed upon his shoulders and they made their way back to the heart of the Golden Community. Neither had seen Toby since.

V

Toby's state of mind, or lack of it, was the result of an accomplishment turned accident; Golden Ones, when free to ponder such matters, conjectured that the meaning of one word was mixed within the meaning of the other, since both shared the same first three letters. Pygmy elders who picked up news often drifting from the Golden Community would chuckle at such verbal antics, remarking "You don't have to look at words to see the connection. Look first to life."

Toby's injuries came about this way. Late in their high school years, Toby and Great Senior wanted to "push open the envelope" of wave surfing, by introducing one little change: to surf at night during the new moon when the sky was clear. They had both heard and adhered to the trilobite legends that the souls of the departed trilobites would ascend from the waters to the "Ocean of Air." The Ocean of Air was a place of reckoning wherein a trilobite reflected on the truthful as well as the errant ways of himself. As insight developed, the less the winds would buffet him this way and that, and he would begin to transcend the Ocean of Air, until he reached the "Ocean of Stars," the greatest ocean of all, a spiritual one, high above the earth. It was a tidy trilobite cosmology; trilobites in material life, however, had only intermittent glimpses of heaven when the sky was clear and the waters calm. That is why few had ever seen the great arthropod constellation that stretched over the seas from horizon to horizon that teachers often talked about in school. Toby and Great Senior then Junior thought surfing the crest of a wave would give them superior advantage in spotting the sparkling souls of trilobites from the past.

On the way for a night time trial run during a new moon, Great Senior then Junior's mind ran as usual in several directions at once. He spoke to Toby of plans for the future. "If we do see more of the stars, we could offer training sessions for the Golden Ones to surf waves at night."

"Uh, huh," Toby murmured. He was half listening,

swimming in the awkward wiggling trilobite way just ahead of Great Senior then Junior. Toby, in the words writ by a being not yet born, was "fat and scant of breath." or at least more so than his companion. Great Senior then Junior was in the habit of vocalizing his thoughts when the audience's attention and exertion, in this instance Toby's, were drawn to other matters.

"Not only is it a strain to swim these waves tonight," thought Toby, "but we have to lift our heads high out of the water to gauge the arrival of swells we want to ride." There was no moonlight to guide their sight and they would have to depend on their sense of hearing. Incessant chatter in the background did not help.

"Do you know what, Toby? I want all trilobites to get in on this. Even the girls. Did you ever notice the girls at school, like Penelope?"

"Oh, uh sort of..." If Toby noticed Penelope at school it was only because she was *like* a girl and belonged with the other girls; there was no particular reason why she should be noticed for any other reason. Toby in these matters thought in the collective mode. Girls only came to the foreground during the molting and the mating, and then once again faded into relative obscurity for another year. In the present moment Toby was busy looking around. Behind them he could hear the waves crashing on the shore near a huge cliff; in front of him was darkness and the sea. Both Toby and Great Senior then Junior handled the swells with ease, but Toby felt them getting stronger.

"I have already been giving her short lessons in agglutination," Great Senior then Junior prattled on. "Have you noticed she just doesn't chomp down on her meals and blindly graze? That is because she is pausing, and in that pause studying what she is eating. She now makes up names for different flavors and colors. Some weeds, she says, will relieve joint pain, others headaches, and so on."

Above, the lightening forked. Both trilobites bobbed up and down. Great Senior seemed lost in a reverie about Penelope. Toby dove a little deeper to enjoy some stillness. He was also trusting his inner sense of timing to come back up just when it would be easiest to catch the large wave he had seen coming in from the distance. Great Senior resumed his babble, thinking his friend was nearby on the surface. "And then there is the way she crawls and moves her tail, with that swing. Gentle, don't you think?...and......*glurgg*!" Great Senior then Junior, not mindful of choppy waters, swallowed some air, gagging as the alien substance made its way down his throat. He ducked beneath the surface again to catch his breath where only gills could retrieve it. He did not see the lightening nor hear the thunder, but crumpled, floating face down, a bit stunned. Later he would claim that neither did he see the hindquarters of Toby scoot past him, his back-legs pushing hard like the oars of an ancient trireme as he sprung to the surface.

It was the most powerful swell that Toby had ever felt, swiftly propelling him into a steep ascent. While his stomach sank, he looked above. There was a large break in the storm clouds. Scattered stars shone serenely in a sable ocean of their own. "I am rising through the Ocean of Air!" Toby cried. He dizzied for a moment, expecting to perch in a celestial berth among the immortals. The crest of the wave then threw him forward with unexpected force, leaving him barely clinging to the edge of the cliff. When lightening flashed, he saw a barren land before him: a horizon beyond which it seemed there were no seas, no balmy coves. A second wave rattled him, upsetting his weak purchase on the cliff, and he fell towards the roiling surf, bouncing off jagged boulders bordering the shore.

Great Senior then Junior did not find his friend until just after after sunrise, when the storm had moved on, far off to those stark regions of nothing but land, which Toby was the first trilobite to view, if only for a moment. There was a zig-zag fault running from the top of Toby's skull down to his upper lip. Great Senior foraged strands of a weed that, according to Penelope, had great binding properties if applied with generous dabs of trilobite spittle. This poultice he applied to Toby's injury with great care. Once certain that Toby was out of immediate danger, he and Penelope made their way back to the Golden Ones, towing their friend, whose steps were slow and uncertain.

The Golden applauded Penelope for the herbal medicine which went far in healing Toby's bodily wounds. But Toby grew in size as he gained strength, which no one could explain, although Penelope guessed a glandular disturbance which no herbal potion in her apothecary could arrest. The remarkable size would not have been a problem were it not for Toby's unpredictable temperament, accompanied with cryptic if not nonsensical utterances. When aroused, he would thrash about the Golden Ones, sometimes at night, frightening especially children. The community finally thought it best Toby be confined, with care, but with little participation in daily trilobite life.

Great Senior then Junior supervised all that was necessary for Toby's seclusion. "You should have everything you need, Friend. The sentinels will be at your beck and call." Toby looked at his friend with his one lucid eye, and Great Senior then Junior thought his meaning had been made clear. But the next day while feigning sleep, Toby stuck a claw out and tripped his friend, to whom he moved closer and whispered: "Can what is within an egg repair the shell so cracked without? Answer but do not shout."

He then dozed off.

VI

It was Great Senior's hope to deliver a welcoming speech for the diverse multitude of trilobites massing towards the Golden Shores, a speech emphasizing the dignity of the great species to which they belonged. No matter that the art of rhetoric had hardly been born or that most of the trilobites could not understand the language of the Golden Ones, or that some of the tribes had no spoken language at all—Great Senior launched himself into composition of his speech several months before the first foreign trilobites began to arrive. Wife and daughter his captive audience, Penelope and Rhonda were fully aware it was impossible to offer advice or attempt to temper Great Senior's enthusiasm, especially in the early and giddy stages of inspiration. They endured many an evening listening to various renditions and arrangements of how trilograms were invented, of the brave Golden Ones who were sent forth to invite alien and unknown tribes, of Penelope's discoveries of healing seaweed poultices, and so on.

"It was a relief," wrote a Pygmy historian in future ages, "that little or no records survive of these attempts at composition. For what we know of the speech at all, it was colossally boring, and would only have survived as an annoyance for future school children to memorize and recite, thus dulling their wits." What had survived was only a phrase, a phrase which led to the collapse of the entire address.

On the evening before the convocation, Great Senior had re-worked the opening of his speech and was trying it out on Penelope and Rhonda, both of whom would have preferred to crouch and vegetate after a sumptuous meal. Great Senior leaned upon a stone used as a podium, and rose himself up before his wife and daughter, cleared his throat, enunciating, "When in the course of trilobitic events, it becomes necessary...etc., etc., etc." Penelope and Rhonda, as they had done each night for the past couple months, smiled approvingly and nodded their heads. It was quite a feat for Great Senior to get so far, for he had no models to build on. There were indeed many pauses, many faltering attempts. As he often forgot or lost his train of thought, he would fumble at the strands tied to his joints, one thread perhaps a hint that would help him recapture his train of thought.

Both wife and daughter were dutiful and devoted in their

attention, but this evening's recital before the convocation was *de trop.* Penelope could not resist turning towards her daughter, whispering, “Psst...doesn’t he mean 'in the *curse* of trilobitic events?'” Rhonda could just suppress a giggle, and then joined her mother in an outburst of laughter, the both of them rolling around on the seabed. “Heee Heee— The *curse* of trilobitic events! The *curse* of trilobitic events! Haww Haww!”

Great Senior went silent, mouth and eyes wide open, slowly tearing the seaweed script of his speech with his fore claws. He felt like an alien, for wife and daughter were huddled now in a space of their own, overflowing with feminine laughter. He fell with a sob to the ground facing away from both of them. Penelope saw him drop first. She paused laughing and crawled towards him, lifting a fore-claw signaling Rhonda to quiet down. Neither she nor her daughter were cruel. She knew her husband's faults. The Great Senior “package” came with a surplus of heart and spirit, but with, too often, a deficit of sense. “Oh, my dear,” she said, gently stroking his antennae with hers, “Don’t weary yourself giving what most are not ready for. The convocation itself is gift enough for now.” Rhonda helped her Mother gently turn him upright. They led him to his bed, where Penelope lay beside him, Rhonda sprawled near his tail. There they persuaded him to drop the speech. It would be enough to have the crowd learn the standard greeting for the convocation, “Hail to thee, ‘tis a trilobite world!” and for the chorus of school children to sing a hymn, followed by demonstrations of the various arts, all of this circumscribed within the advent of the crowd molting and mating.

Rhonda and Penelope began to clip and discard the strands of mnemonic seaweed so thick and clustered about the joints of all his legs. Great Senior was a bit too proud to confess to his wife that the mowing had eased the strain of his movement, but both she and Rhonda saw him smile. They also scoured his shell. He rose the morning of the convocation well-rested and refulgent, at first hardly recognized by the sentinels who escorted him to the amphitheater, marveling now at his youthful appearance.

VII

For a year before the convocation, work crews had hollowed out an amphitheater in an area just off the shoreline. The amphitheater sloped more or less evenly into the depths. Great Senior's podium was at the shallow end of the waters. Rows in arcs of ever increasing size spread from the shallows into the darker waters. There was room for thousands of trilobites. Teams of Golden Ones had escorted the visitors to their appropriate seating areas, keeping each trilobite neighbor to another of the same color. The first rows were reserved for the Golden, the very first for the school children. In the rows beyond the Golden were the Silver, and then the Grey, the Mottled, the Bronze, and the Blue. The furthest and deepest rows held a contingent of the Albinos, as they were sensitive to sunlight and could not approach closer except during the night.

The sun broke though a thin cloud layer when Great Senior mounted the podium. He first saw the Albinos crawl back, then return with the cloud cover. It was a massive assembly, but quiet, as they had just been fed not more than an hour ago; the ballast of full stomachs pulled them towards the ground. Great Senior surveyed the school children before him, who looked back with a devoted and expectant air as if they were in class. They had been tutored daily for weeks in their task, which was to ignite from their tiny spark of enthusiasm, expansive and buoyant spirit to engulf the multitude.

Great Senior lifted his fore claws. “Hail to thee, friends!”

The children returned in unison what they had endlessly practiced in school: “'Tis a trilobite world!”

Great Senior stepped off the podium and touched the foreheads of each child with his antennae. Then the children turned to the row behind them, giving them the salutation. Each row in turn did the same. As the salutation reached the rows of visitors furthest from the Golden Shores, the responses grew more halting with fewer voices. Several repetitions were needed to bring them into full harmony and rhythm with the whole.

After the Albinos in the last row chimed in, Great Senior again climbed up his podium. “'Tis a trilobite world! 'Tis a trilobite world! 'Tis a trilobite world!" he shouted. The crowd repeated the phrase with the same fervor.

A small trilobite scuttled up the aisle from his seat—the blue trilobite child Great Senior had startled the morning of the day before. Now bold and spirited, the young fellow approached Great Senior. “Hail to thee, friend!” the fellow chirped.

Great Senior chuckled, picked him up, lifting him above

his forehead. "'Tis a trilobite world!" The hundreds who had learned this incantation in the past couple of days replied, much to the satisfaction of those tribes who had already a great sophistication in a spoken tongue. But even those without followed their fellow trilobites in scraping the sea floor with their hind and fore claws in an instinctive reflex of delight and approval.

Great Senior set down the little blue trilobite. The Golden school children welcomed him to a place in their row, a gesture which quickly warmed Great Senior, feeling within success of the convocation. It was now time for the hymn. He motioned for the crowd to quiet down. He turned again to the children with one fore claw as a conductor's baton. The children began to sing:

A mighty fortress are we arthropods,
A bulwark never failing;
Tho' waves may tumble.
The sea floor rumble.
Ever stable in our shells
Are we-ee-eee!

The hymn, first line of which was also the title, Great Senior had written several years ago when emerging inspired from a state of deep agglutination. In contemplation, he had grasped what he believed to be the very essence of trilobite being: its shell. There were to his mind no other creatures like the trilobites in the sea, and indeed on the seabed, for what would the sea be without its bottom, and what would life be without the crowning creatures called the trilobites? Much later, some Pygmies would contend that the shell was something of a burden. What after all did the trilobite leave behind when it died? And how could the souls ascend to the starry heavens if the shell was not left behind? Yet Great Senior would have argued that what it left behind was perhaps greater than what it was going to: the shell was perhaps an image of the Eternal on Earth. The shining soul could have its heaven, but the shell *belonged* on Earth, endowing the Earth with a special character, emanating from its most exceptional inhabitants.

The singing voices became fainter, trailing off into what was an uneasy silence for Great Senior, for he, the lyricist, knew the song had at least two more stanzas. Great Senior opened his eyes. The little ones were looking upward and beyond him, as if mesmerized. Great Senior craned his neck and strained his eyes towards the underside of the water's surface: myriads of tiny silver and white specks sparkled in the wavy sunlight. Each was motile, alive and twirling, yet held in a group that formed a shifting cloud, moving away from the convocation, weightless and fairy-like in texture.

The children's chorus began to break up their disciplined rows, some already scuttling past Great Senior himself without so much as even a nod goodbye or glance of respect or recognition. “Damn offspring of the All Flowing!” the startled Great Senior muttered to himself. The “All Flowing” were the jellyfish who populated ocean waters long before the trilobites rose to preeminence. They were silent and peaceful, and in no ways a threat to the trilobites, except that the trilobite young were fascinated with the loose, diaphanous and sometimes sun or moonlit saturated garments of these creatures. It happened more often than once that a young trilobite would wander off following an All Flowing, and never return.

This was happening now. Great Senior feared for the children, and began to sing a didactic rhyme taught in school, a rhyme he himself formulated, encapsulating the very essence of trilobite being:

> The All Flowing are sparkling and pretty,
> But life is iffy be you soft and squishy.
> Oh, wouldn't you rather be
> A pair of ragged claws
> That drag on the bottom of the sea,
> Like me?

At this point he danced a *pirouette* while humming the tune. Each recital of the verse was heartfelt by Great Senior. The verses had been so effective in school that no Golden children had been reported following a jellyfish since Great Senior introduced the song shortly before he had conceived of the Great Convocation. School children would often beg him to recite it when he visited their classes, but now it was as if none of the chorus had ever been to school. The older Golden Ones seated behind the chorus, who first picked up their heads when they heard the verse, were breaking up their rows, following the sparkling cloud floating further and further beyond. The sentinels who were trained to keep order abandoned their posts, transfixed by the wisps of light pulsing above the gathering.

Great Senior moved from his podium towards these clusters breaking away from the convocation. "Stop!" he cried. "Its just a minor interruption. It'll soon pass. The sentinels shall bring them back, surely." Undaunted, he recited the verse again, but in a louder voice, while swaying back and forth, clicking his fore claws as if they were castanets. He grinned as he twirled around.

Great Senior danced well, but he was out of sync with the masses whom just moments before he meant to instruct and to lead. Some registered the mounting bustle and knocking about as signals that molting and mating were about to begin. After a third go at the dance and the verse, Great Senior stumbled over shells of the rapidly dis-armoring trilobites. who now moved beside him and around him, anticipating to merge their soft, fleshy forms in amorous embraces. Great Senior was but a rock in their way.

Crowds now clambering down to the first rows and beyond, in search of level ground to abandon their shells, bumped Great Senior left and right. A few loose shells kicked aside in the confusion also hit him. He fell backward, half-sunk in the sand. There were no sentinels around to assist him. He struggled to his feet, clinging to the podium, leaning forward to brace and balance himself. In profile, he resembled a statue, perhaps of a knight weary in defeat, now retired into himself immobile, surrounded by the ghostly white wraiths creeping about the ocean floor, seeking for partners, their armor scattered and abandoned around them.

"Is this the trilobite world without me?" he asked of himself. He and Penelope had conceived their Rhonda during a molting period, as had all trilobites, but in a space apart and askew to the Golden masses. The agglutinated needed a territory, however small, of their own, a reservoir of instinct apart from the whole, shaped and bounded through their individuality. Love could not mean anything if it did not mean: "I love *you*," as he recalled saying those many molting and mating seasons ago. He glanced beyond the connubial trilobites towards the now broken sand ridges that had made up the amphitheater. There were no laborers weeping over its destruction or bemoaning the fate of wasted effort. He could linger no more. He turned as if to leave, perhaps meander his way back home where the stings of remorse might be softened, even assuaged. But he felt a trembling pass through his shell, then repeat itself. He paused, sensing they were not the reactions of instinctual desire awakening from a long dormancy within. The source was outside: tremors of earth. Such quakes he recalled from his childhood in which not a small number of the Golden slid into deep and sandy graves. Yet how fortunate were those now scattered about him, he mused, whom passion rendered insensible to imminent death!

The trembling though, did not spread much beyond the small patch of earth surrounding him. A voice, first faint, arose from the depths growing louder as it approached the surface:

Lose weight,
Shed that crate
Get ready to mate
To hell with the shell
'Cause if you carry that freight
You can't create!

Toby burst forth in glory, surrounded by billows of sand. A shaken Great Senior fell on Toby's forehead, tumbling on to the back of his old friend's shell. Great Senior grabbed the remnants of seaweed twine that were still attached to Toby's leg joints and held fast. Great Senior recognized the weave: It was the twine he had given Longinus. Toby plowed through the ruins of the amphitheater, scattering the many shells and bruising not a few couples who could not figure what had hit them.

"Toby....Toby...its me," gasped Great Senior, "Your old......friend."

"Toby or not Toby? That is the question. O my little Ahab. Little, only because the first to bear that name! What a mess a later one shall make. Larger and later. But you—maybe not so bad!"

He turned towards the deep with his cargo towards the abode of the Albinos. Those of the trilobites scattered about, soon to rest from ardor spent, still wrapped within one another's tender flesh, may have heard Toby's fading voice, as he and his cargo sped into the cooler and darker waters.

O, to Hell with the shell!
Give freedom to your back
Let your belly swell,
Let your old crate crack.
Let your bellies slap
Lend a bend to the back
Let your old crate crack ....

VIII

Penelope wove most of the day in a quiet spot near the roots of her Sargasso garden. When she saw the sun's waving rays grow slant, she rose to the surface, for it was well past time for the convocation to have ended. She expected to see the core of the agglutinated ones passing by on their way home: among them Great Senior arriving, surrounded by a clutch of admirers, and Rhonda arm in arm with Longinus. Rhonda did not hesitate to admit to her mother that without the return of Longinus, she would have ditched the convocation all together. Toby, Penelope recalled much to her relief, was to be quartered some distance away with the sentinels who would ensure he wasn't a bother.

Those whom she first saw, however, were coming from a direction opposite the amphitheater: the sentinels with the schoolchildren, all of them exhausted, but rescued, no longer enchanted by guile of their pied pipers. A senior sentinel told Penelope of the surprise appearance of the All Flowing, the break up of the chorus, and the pursuit to save them. None had witnessed Toby's upheaval. Penelope, with a knowing chuckle and a smile wife-craft wise, so sensitive to the foibles and ways of her husband, said, “Oh my! He never could stand them. I just hope he didn't make a fool of himself, the poor dear. You know, once he caught sight of them just as we were...” The sentinels politely interrupted, begging her permission to leave as they had to return the children to their parents.

She could not refuse them. Now alone again, she glanced in the direction of the amphitheater, although it was out of sight. She recalled that you only had to mention the All Flowing to provoke her husband's ire, to which he would add a diatribe against the poor creatures even more fulsome than the convocation address he had practiced for so long. It could be a long evening once he arrived home.

She saw the agglutinated Golden parents straggling past with their children in hand, only a few waving salutation to her. It was as if they did not want to talk to her at all. Why should they look so sad and worn? Had her husband's speech been that long? As the darkness approached, the last figure she saw was Rhonda, bent and crawling slowly towards her with a child trilobite. It was the blue boy of a distant tribe who had first poked his head into Great Seniors doorway; the boy who enthusiastically shouted "'Tis a trilobite world!" when Great Senior lifted him high above his shoulders. He too was tempted to follow the All Flowing, but Rhonda grabbed him just in time. Although he was not a child of the agglutinated Golden, he was all she could retrieve from the debacle about her, Toby having dragged her father as quickly, it seemed, as he had discarded Longinus.

Rhonda recounted the mishaps of the convocation, not going beyond the question mark punctuating the crisis: what became of her father, her lover, and Toby? Penelope bent towards the child; while cradling one forearm about him, picking up bits of seaweed for him to nibble. The blue boy eagerly took to her nurturing as he would have from any other kind trilobite. He looked at her with bright eyes while babbling to himself what few words he had learned earlier in the day, now probably completely forgotten.

Rhonda wept. Penelope looked beyond her daughter: "Now you give so freely, Daughter, of what is our All Flowing. Trilobite tears made this sea our home."

Pygmy historians maintained firmly that Longinus, although dazed and injured, made it back to the Golden Shores. Meditating upon the ruins of the amphitheater and the loss of Great Senior, Longinus resolved that he and Rhonda would rather have a pregnancy among the Pygmies, who greatly savored Penelope's utterances, calling them the greatest *sutras* in the language of the Golden Shores. But Golden trilobites ridiculed this belief, regarding her remarks as being wholly out of character for a Golden One, and hardly in keeping with the celebratory nature of the Great Convocation and all others that followed. Simply, tears were not "good for business."

IX

Sam and Abner spent that morning of the Great Convocation "doing the flick," a traditional game of the Albinos, indeed their favorite pastime. A small hole was dug, sometimes one, two, or three body-lengths away from a predetermined line behind which the players stood, attempting to flick stones to fill the hole. The player with the most stones in won the game. Today, Sam, the shorter of the two, lay down to measure the distance to the hole. Tomorrow would be Abner's turn. Abner, the more skilled flicker, was winning despite the shorter distance. Sam was not bothered; it was, after all, just a game. Besides why waste leisure time in a foul mood? That would be bad form. He and Abner had been very good sports in volunteering to "mind the store" while the rest of the Albinos scampered off to the Great Convocation. The "store" was the territory which bordered the Great Abyss, that treacherous drop-off into incalculable depths from which no creature was ever seen to arise.

"Doing the flick" resembled the chief activity of the Albinos, their main service to the trilobite species at large, for they undertook care of the deceased whom they disposed of by slipping them into the Abyss, with a bit more ceremony, however, than just flicking stones. Albinos, by custom, offered two types of burials. The plainest honored only the shell. Family or friends of the deceased were expected to remove the softer portions and place them in a shallow grave. The deluxe alternative involved shoving the entire corpse into the Abyss. Each method appealed to different temperaments. Those who lingered in grief preferred to watch the shell as it drifted slowly downwards, wafting about like a falling leaf, until out of sight. Others of a more stoic nature preferred the loud plunge and rapid descent of mortal remains, evoking death's abrupt erasure, the impermanence that haunts all things.

Abner was especially fascinated by the deluxe spectacle, although the hardier trilobites who chose it were in the minority. “You can see the family and friends standing there. Each feels the beating of his heart in his breast, but when they gaze downward into the waters, there is nothingness!” This thought and its many implications he wanted to write down, but couldn't as he hadn't learned how. He heard the rumors of trilograms and seaweed script being taught at the Great Convocation; this was his only regret in not attending. However, the bright sunlight of the Golden Shores would probably fatigue his eyes, and the dark of deeper waters would frustrate any Golden One offering to teach him the skills involved, or so he reasoned. He stayed behind to demonstrate the only art he had mastered.

He had invented a maneuver all his own, called the “backward flick,” which now, only one stone away from winning, he attempted. The flick was made with hind legs, the player facing away from the hole.

“Ah, winning point!" he said, turning around to see the top of the stone poking out of the depression.

“Good shot! Never saw you miss one, yet!” said the amiable Sam, never to begrudge excellence when he saw it. “Let's take a break. Maybe walk along the Abyss. I'm a bit tired of flicking.”

“I am not surprised. Most of your stones missed the hole. Your game was spent mostly running after them. I even think one went into the Abyss, tsk tsk.” Abner would only gloat a bit. He agreed to a short walk along that ridge.

The stretch of sea floor, usually busy with mourners coming and going, and Albinos dragging a shell or the whole arthropod, was now deserted and silent. The edge of the drop-off, usually riddled with the impressions made by trilobite remains daily discarded, had now become soft, currents slowly shifting the sand.

"Think of what this place will be like and what we'll see when our friends return from the Great Convocation!" Sam mused aloud after several minutes of silent crawling. Having only handled the corpses of the Golden and sometimes of the Silver, and little traveled beyond the drop off, he could only imagine the deceased of the Bronze, the Scarlet, or the Speckled. The dusky Pygmy seemed to him the most exotic in coloration and size. Sam thought that business along the Abyss would increase as members of these alien tribes, unfamiliar with the temperature shifts and seaweeds of the Golden Shores, might fail to acclimatize and fall ill. The Golden would be poor hosts if they did not bring the remains of their unfortunate guests to the Albinos for a proper burial.

"You may be right," replied Abner, the elder of the two, who had seen much more. "But weak trilobites often pass away early on a long journey. I think the ones who made it to the convocation are the fittest. Some of them have their own rites and customs to handle the dead. I don't think they would have dragged them to the Golden Shores".

"Won't there be a lot of shells there anyway, because of the molting? Maybe our buddies will bring some of these back as souvenirs?"

"You might be right there. We'll see."

They grew silent again. Sam, although largely nonathletic, had mastered a walk in which he would weave toward the drop off and kick sand into the depths by moving all of his legs at once on that side, and then suddenly weave back, all feet on solid sand. He did this quickly, moving a bit beyond Abner who was peering into the distance.

"Hey, Sam! Wait a minute. Take a look ahead. Do you see what I see?"

Sam halted. Plowing towards the ridge of the Abyss was a huge Golden, leaving a long trail of sand swirling in the water behind him. Sam and Abner marveled at the size and speed. Whoever it was did not slow down as it approached the Abyss. "Looks like someone who is going to 'shelf his own shell,'" Abner remarked: a common euphemism for a trilobite taking his own life.

But this was not an act of suicide born out of despair. Rather it was like the elephant of modern times, who sensing the approach of life's end, would separate from the herd and search out the jungle graveyard of his kind, there to fall to rest midst hallowed ivory monuments of his ancestors. The Golden Ones did not have a such a graveyard besides the Abyss. The one approaching his doom would often go off alone, although it was common for family members to follow him until the end. Abner had seen this several times before. What was strange was that this one appeared alone. The Golden One stopped right at the edge of the drop off. When the clouds of sand settled, Sam and Abner could see the hulk stuck and silent.

"His heart must have given out so he couldn't lift himself over."

Sam slowly turned his gaze from head to tail of the humongous Golden. Even in the light of shadowy waters the shell was brighter than any he had seen before. In the weak light, the mass of seaweed on top of his shell might mirage into the shape of another trilobite.

"We gotta help this poor fellow out, Sam. Let's get around his hind end and see if we can't flick him over with a few backward kicks." So they positioned themselves. Sam wondered again at the golden hue. "Well, get thee behind me, Suntan," He laughed at his own joke as he got into position.

"OK." said Abner. "On the count of three: one...two..."

The nudge startled Toby, whose back legs snapped back, throwing the Albinos on the sea floor. "Is this the shove that moves the sun and other stars?"

Unsteady are the traces
We leave in Earthly places
So thus I beetle o'er my bases...

Toby intoned as he slid into the Abyss.

Abner remembered these lines, repeating them silently to himself at each funeral act he performed till the end of his life. Like Abner, Sam did not know exactly what the words meant, but he liked their sounds, reciting them too when it came time to send Abner's shell on its way.

X

Great Senior gazed upward, the surface of the sea growing more distant and dim. Yet the depths were tranquil. There was little to fear on this journey downward. But what about the destination?

"Toby, are we going to crash?"

"There are no crashes here. The fall is eternal. This is Paradise, for a trilobite world."

* * *

PURGATORIO

Then came we down upon the desert shore,
Which never yet saw navigate its waters
Any that afterward had known return.
Dante

Elmo paddled almost silently in the water, with Smudge bobbing right behind him, both approaching the shore of that unexplored land beyond. Was that land as vast as the sea the trilobites now swam in? Elmo didn't know, and neither did Smudge, and neither did their teachers, who offered inconclusive and contradictory theories about what lay beyond the waters. It was only certain that the ravines and valleys stretched from the present to the time of that first, the Great Convocation, and even further back. The trilobites had now been on earth for so long that the living would find fossilized remains and traces of their ancestors. Children at school recited a poem composed by a trilobite bard celebrating this discovery:

We praise that first trilobite,
Name to us unknown
So sturdy with pluck,
Who first bore the shock
Of finding a face like his own
Staring out from a rock.

Smudge and Elmo, known as the "fossil boys" of

Golden Shores, would scout for their treasures on weekends or holiday outings, bringing them for other students to admire and envy. The other students were less keen at spotting key fossil features half-hidden, protruding from the sea floor. Smudge thought this weekend would be like any other, great fossil finds or no, but Elmo surprised him with a new adventure. "Yes," Elmo whispered not wishing to be overheard, especially by parents or teachers, clutching the shoulder of his friend. "We will go out swimming near the shore as usual, but now with eyes focused beach-ward, on the lookout for a UTC!" A UTC was an "Unidentified Terrestrial Creature." Saturday morning, Elmo took off towards the shore knowing that "stick-in-the-mud" Smudge would finally follow stuttering "b-b-b-buts," and so he did, swimming through the cloud of sand Elmo kicked up behind, and swallowing some of it.

The UTC craze had been going on for some time. Reports came in about tiny, quick creatures scurrying around near the shore. As these observations were often made by weak-eyed seniors tipsy from nibbling a prehistoric locoweed, some reports were less convincing than others. But they stimulated the imagination of the trilobite population. A falling leaf or a stone rolling down hill were evidence enough to suggest an apocalyptic invasion of land creatures, or the fulfillment of a millennial yearning for beings unknown who would pour milk and honey in trilobite mouths, well-fed but dulled by a monotonous diet. Some claimed that meeting such beings would herald a new epoch in the destiny of life on Earth, perhaps introducing creatures supplanting the Golden Ones themselves: the aliens may have detailed knowledge of the strengths and weaknesses of the trilobite physiology and exploit them for their advantage.

As scant the real evidence was for such conjecture, fears and expectations about UTC's grew, undermining confidence in the "Golden Establishment," much to the alarm of the elders who made it up. A cult counter to the Great Convocation sprung up, with an altar to "The Unknown Terrestrials." The cult maintained that these created the Golden Ones, consigning them to the lesser element of water. The cult was of course a threat to the *trilo-centric* point of view, the epicenter of which was Golden Shores, which spread its influence throughout Devonian waters.

Yet the trilobite elders were wise enough not to suppress the cult or enforce standard orthodoxy in such a way as to provoke hardened resistance and quite possibly an "underground" rebellion that might go on for generations. As the young were most infatuated with the land as a tempting alternative to the waters, the elders employed story tellers that portrayed trilobites entering that alien territory through a cunning and ingenuity that only the water-bound trilobite could possess.

The bards and story-tellers who versified the hero trilobites past, such as Great Senior or the unnamed finder of the first fossil, now began composing tales including in some way the UTC's. These tales were popular among the school-aged trilobites like Elmo and Smudge. The most popular series of tales concerned a trilobite named Terry, and his gang of "Terranauts," a group who had discovered, through special exercises and technological innovations, a way of surviving and thriving in a non-aquatic environment. Special exercises included calisthenics, and a supplemental diet of minerals would strengthen shells, which would be oiled to retard the loss of moisture. The technological advances included burrowing tunnels which held water and allowed the trilobites to journey deep into the land by going underneath. Burrows could easily turn into rivers by removing the dirt overhead and throwing it aside. UTC's, when they appeared, were almost always malign or threatening types who attempted to subvert the inland advance of trilobite society.

Tales of Terry and the Terranauts were eventually dramatized in serial fashion, an episode usually performed at the end of the school week. Elmo and Smudge had just seen the latest play, in which Terry and his gang had burrowed into a small underground body of water. There they discovered a lost tribe of trilobites who had been cut off from the Golden Shore trilobites by an earthquake, and whose existence had been long forgotten.

This was the first of the dramatized tales to include a major role for a female, although Terry remained the dominant figure. Nonetheless, the character of Teresa, companion and confidante to Terry, signaled a break with the canonical standards of the many terranaut sagas. A pert girl played the role of Teresa, who captured Elmo's fancy. His desire to find a UTC was mixed with a wish to find a Princess Teresa, or to at least be admired by one. Actually, the attentions of a neighborhood girl would have done, but anyone less than what his imagination conceived would have been too mundane.

Elmo and Smudge were raised in families with traditional trilobitic beliefs that were simple and clear. There was the water, there was land, and above both, the heavens, the abode of trilobites deceased, shining lights for future generations. A trilobite never left the sea of life, and never crossed into another realm until the moment of death when shell and soft parts were ceded to sea floor and the Abyss. The soul rose to heaven, joining a "stellarized" community. Traditionalists argued that the UTC story tellers had denatured these cherished beliefs, infecting the minds of the young with notions of “other worlds” beyond the sea. Some even argued they interfered with the “natural stability” of the trilobite, that tendency towards steady shell-weighted ballast honored by the Great Senior.

Elmo’s parents did allow their son the freedom to enjoy a weekly session with the story tellers and their dramas. Yet they made sure he reinforce “stability” by reciting every night and morning the most important *sutra* of the trilobite code:

Properly shod
Is the arthropod
For the sea floor,
And nothing more.

His parents saw him go off with Smudge this Saturday morning as they had so many before, not thinking mischief would be afoot just ahead of their “properly shod” son.

Elmo and Smudge had already been on the hunt for

hours; it was now close to noon. They moved in towards the shore on the morning tide, and easily rode the gentle swells, moving along the shoreline. Observation was easy, not having to struggle against currents and tire themselves out to keep their orientation. While Elmo relished conditions affording such ease in searching, the same conditions bored Smudge. If they were fossil hunting as usual, they would have already picked up a bundle. Plus there was always the chance of finding a tidbit of fresh seaweed to nibble. The weed in shallower waters was less crisp, sometimes soft, and rotted quickly in the sunlight. Smudge's eyes hurt, and his back legs cramped from lack of moving about.

"There's nothing on the shore, Elmo. Besides, I'm hungry."

"Sir Terranaut, you do mistake me. My name is *Terry.*"

"O....well, Sir Whoever....I'm going back where it's deeper. To cool my back. Get something to eat."

"Giving up so quickly? The UTC are wary critters to be sure. Have they worn ya down so soon? They think they're clever hiding from us. Takes patience to be a trekker. Gotta even be even tougher to be a *terranaut.* Don't you remember the story about the Great Senior's granddaughter caught in the mud tunnel during an earthquake...and how the terranaut saved her? An' what happened when the tunnel almost collapsed? And..." Elmo did not see Smudge wander back to deeper waters.

"Its not just a story." Elmo continued. "I bet I can burrow right up to the shore closer to open land than I have ever been before. Maybe closer than any trilobite has!....Except maybe......" He and Smudge had once caught a whiff of a rotting trilobite rolling in the shoreline surf earlier one time when fossil hunting. Memory of the odor slowed him down for a bit, but the fantasy of being a terranaut was irrepressible. He imagined that he was Terry burrowing a new tunnel to rescue the granddaughter of the legendary Great Senor and Penelope, the granddaughter thought missing after a storm pushed her to shore. Terry brought her home to the Golden Ones just as a ceremony to mourn her death was about to begin. The Great Convocation celebrated his heroism; Great Senior and Penelope could not refuse him their daughter's hand in marriage. The story teller showed great economy in the narrative, for the rescue occurred only several days before the Great Convocation, one event lending its energy to next, culminating in romantic union. For Elmo this arrangement was not artifice, but how things should be. Imagination excelled in portraying them so; so why not equally powerful in making them so? He fancied he just missed a trilobite girl by happenstance wandering past him who might witness his imminent achievement, filling her with admiration. Assuming she was there, Elmo 's chest swelled with bravado.

He let the gentle surf take him towards the shore; when he was just covered by water, he bent his head towards the sand beneath him. He moved forward, the sand piled up around his head, and he was a little deeper than he was before. He continued, going deeper until his head was covered with sand. Resting for a moment, he borrowed further again until he was completely covered. Some grains smarted his gills and stuck in his throat, making him cough, but he could bear it. He lifted his head just enough to break out of the burrow and felt his eyes staring at the ground just beyond the water. "Hey, Smudge! Look at me!" But Smudge did not hear him. He was either under water searching for grub, at home, or on his way there. A sea breeze sharply stung Elmo's eyes; he plunged his head into the muddy water. He figured he would have to do this repeatedly if he wanted to search the shore for a UTC. Funny—neither Terry nor his Terranauts had this problem. The story-tellers never spoke of it.

Elmo was just up to where the water lapped on the shore; he wanted Smudge's applause as much as he wanted to chide him for being a sluggard and maybe a coward. But the call of the UTC's beckoned him, and Elmo would continue until he found one, or at least traces of one which he could whip up into convincing evidence. Then he could wow school chums on Monday morning. Smudge crouched in the background with downcast eyes. Lifting his head once more from the muddy water, Elmo turned his gaze towards the shore sand. Tiny black dots caught up in the surf would roll in the sand when the water receded, but then scatter about all on their own.

Peering more closely, Elmo found each dot had a rounded black shell, even smaller heads with feelers, and legs sticking out on both sides. "Smudge!" he shouted. "The UTC's! I've found them! Right here! *They're just like us*!!" He gently shoved wet sand to make a small pool to let several bugs swirl about. One crawled up his right fore claw, pausing for a moment, moving its feelers. Elmo half-expected him to talk, but himself attempted verbal contact. "Hail to thee, friend, 'tis a trilobite world!" The ancient salutation sprung forth spontaneously in Elmo's loudest voice, startling the beetle, who jumped, poking Elmo in the eye, scurrying across its surface.

Elmo writhed and whined in pain, shaking his head in the shallow water to wash the bug off his eye. But the beetle's company followed his suit, jumping from Elmo's left claw into the left eye. He furiously dipped his head again and again into the little pool, and choked on the mud. For a moment he paused, mostly clear of the bugs, but found his back, now exposed to sun and air, was heating up.

The tide was going out. He felt his insides tighten like cord. His mouth, too, was getting dry, but the pool had also shrunk and he could barely wet his gills, now burning in the sunlight. "I had better go back. No terranaut is a coward for knowing his limits," he gasped to himself. True enough. And this was not a bit of dialogue remembered and recited from the story-tellers' stock of heroic quotables.

He attempted to pull himself back, but his legs flailed about in the air. He heard the sweet sound of sea waves behind him, unreachable. Never did his weight feel so much a burden as it did now. The beetles returned, exploring his skull, climbing his antennae, and crawling over the vast territory of his back. Elmo thought he heard them giggling, having great sport in exploring this new world, his body.

"We gotcha, we gotcha!" Other voices called from behind him, but he ached so, and could not turn around.

Someone or something had lifted his back legs, pulling him into the water and the healing waves. With seared eyes soothed, and gills now in full white and pink bloom, he heard Smudge say, "Close call, buddy!" Elmo felt the sure grip of his friend.

But not Smudge alone. It took more than one trilobite to yank Elmo away from the land, for more than one trilobite cared for him. They all formed a golden chain from the shore down into the depths that led to his home: his parents and Smudge's, other friends from school, his school teachers: Smudge had called them all.

The last he called were the story-tellers who abandoned their song and sagas, heeding the call of real pain to save a real life. At the very end of the chain, when all broke to celebrate, Elmo saw Princess Teresa. He called out to her by that name. She gave Elmo a half-smile. "If I didn't like you, I wouldn't mind you calling me that."

* * *

INFERNO

Their eyes, which first were only moist within
Gushed o'er the eyelids, and the frost congealed
Their tears between and locked them up again.
Dante

Tiktaalik *fils*, stuck in the middle of a school of fish that had crept up on him, stammered politely in what little he knew of the common fish dialect, "Excuse me!Tetrapod on your left! Tetrapod on your left! Could I please just go ahead?" This, although gurgled in the best accent he could muster, went unnoticed. "Fish come, fish go," His father once said. "The fish ye shall always have with thee. They travel in schools which you hope to avoid." His father had told him him the trick of diving beneath or swimming above a school, provided you didn't do it too late, but the son did not practice, and had forgotten the advice. Tiktaalik *pere* was now ahead of his son and patiently waiting for him below the mass of silver bodies that eventually would have to pass by. Tiktaalik *fils* plodded along as best he could. He thought fish were dumb, even the colorful ones, and to him seemed frozen in place, as well as in face, for they wore the same gaping mouthed expression. Although they were always in school, they learned very little, except perhaps only how to stay in school.

How unlike fish were the Tiktaaliks! They had four legs,

could move about on the beaches or the land, their bodies sporting lungs for the former, and gills for the latter. Titaaliks also had necks. Motile and more pliable than their finny neighbors, Tiktaaliks were as adept at expressing their inner selves as they were in exploring the outer realms around them and sampling many delights.

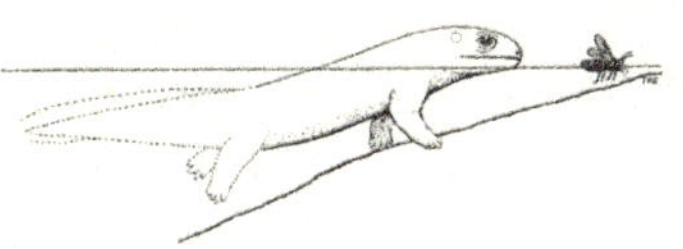

Tiktallik *fils* was a wit. One morning his parents asked him to wake up Tiktaalik *soeur* so she wouldn't be late to school. He did so, coming back with his mouth stretched open wide in fish fashion, and said in a deep voice, "I am sorry to say, she has seen too much land," that being the euphemism fish used for describing one of their kind who had died. His parents chuckled, warning him not to practice his mimicry in front of fish, especially in a funeral gathering. The humor, though, was perfectly acceptable among their own kind.

II

"What is the oldest name for this stretch of beach?" Tiktaalik *pere* asked his son. They had just arrived, Tiktaalik *fils* a bit wearily, where they were going to take a dive, something his father promised earlier in the week. Tiktaalik *pere* said the dive would be deeper than the other dives they had taken together, and that they would see a great achievement of the trilobite civilization which his son was presently studying in school. Tiktaalik *fils,* panting still a little too quickly, sputtered an answer.

"Uh, the Golden Beach?" he offered, remembering something mentioned about this at school.

His father smiled and nodded yes. "Golden because of what?" he asked further.

Easy, thought his son. "Because the trilobites have Golden shells."

"Great! Now, is there any other reason why these trilobites are called Golden?"

Tiktaalik *fils* stalled. He had no answer. Colors didn't make much of a difference to him. There were fish more colorful than tiktaaliks, but nobody would want to be a tiktaalik on the basis of color alone. So what was so special about gold? "Gee, I dunno, Dad." he replied.

"Well, don't mind. You're going to find out soon enough. Take a plunge!" As his son went under. Tiktaalik *pere* looked up at the sky. It was partly cloudy; there was the chance that the view he was hoping for would not overwhelm his son, as it had his mother years ago when Tiktaalik *pere* dove with her on a first date. She still talked about that. She would often say to her friends, "I knew he was good as gold from that moment on." Sometimes a tear would drop from an obsidian eye.

It was a long way down for Tiktaalik *fils;* his father was glad to see that his son was sharp to empty all the air from his lungs, "kick-starting" his gills, thus easing the descent. The water was clear, but without rays of sunlight guiding them until just before they lit. Tiktaalik *fils* found himself tilted with the legs on one side sunk in the sand, and the opposite raised up on a high and hard surface, radiant gold in color. The entire surface was wide and long, wandering into the distance, covering small valleys and hills. Sunlight put the road in high and sharp relief against the muted colors of the water and the seabed. The vegetation diminished as the road became dominant in its glory, even as it receded into the distance, following the seashore in its own winding way.

The road was as spectacular in detail as it was in the whole, made of the shells of golden trilobites carefully laid and fitted together.

"It took thousands of years to build. A kind of cement, made from trilobite spittle mixed with sea floor sand, binds all the shells together. Only if hundreds of thousands of golden trilobites were involved would there be enough spittle to build such a road."

"Did they kill to get the shells?"

"No. The trilobites believed that what they couldn't take to the great beyond, they should leave behind in some constructive way. It took hundreds of generations to leave their shells. Would have been quite a mess on the ground otherwise, especially for those who can't swim, including the trilobites, who don't really swim that well."

"Where does the road go? Where does it begin?"

Tiktaalik *fils* began to run up the low hill before them. It delighted him that the hard but smooth surface supported his feet, which would otherwise sink in sand, slowing his way. When he was on top of the hill, he collapsed with a smile on his face, heart beating wildly.

"You had better rest up before we swim to the surface. I want to go down into the valley ahead to look for some sea-flowers for your mother. I won't be long." Tiktaalik *pere* recalled a field of sea-flowers when he first dove with his son's mother. It was a bit naive to suppose the field still blossomed. Sea-flowers were favored either as food or as decoration among the trilobites as well as the tiktaaliks, and as the field was so close to the "trib" highway, it had probably been picked out.

Tiktaalik *fils* lay belly down in the golden aura of the road. He thought it magnificent, but somehow strange that such an impressive structure was built by creatures, well, clunky and ugly. Was this the meaning his father was getting at? Was this why the trilobites were golden in other ways than their shells?

Tiktaalik *pere* found the fields bare of flowers; he plod on, hoping to find some other gift for his wife, when he reached a pile of stones marking the boundary where the Golden Realm ended, and that of the Silver Trilobites began. He pushed forward a bit. The road he noticed began losing its shine, and the surface was littered with a black and brown, sometimes oily grit; the silt thickened as he progressed, finally up to his knee joints. He came across an adult trilobite main shell tipped over and scoured out. Shell pieces of legs, the forearms, and the massive head helmet lay scattered just off the side of the road. Beyond these remnants on either side, he saw hundreds of shells overturned, and further on ahead, the golden road itself blocked by piles of shells. He struggled to reach them.

They too, were scoured, some with remnant strings of flesh waving in the slow current of the foul water, the taste of which made him gag and withdraw.

Once back at the boundary point, he stopped and raised his head. The sun on the water's surface quivered as if alive, so alien it seemed from this eerie and funereal place. The homeland of the Silver Trilobites, emptied! How? Tiktaalik *pere* did not know. "My boy...I don't want him to see this."

The calm face of his son touched his heart when he reached the top of the hill. Tiktaalik *fils* said, "That gold color really does get to you after awhile, doesn't it? Thanks Pop, for bringing me here. Hey, where are the sea flowers?"

"Weren't any. Just a romantic fool thinking there would be," the father speaking more to his absent wife than to his son right before him. "Say, why don't we go to the top and hit the beach. We can surprise your mother with some of those tiny beetles she likes so much."

"OK. But wouldn't it be great if we had a way to bring back some gold?"

He let his son shoot upwards first, towards the light and fresh air—more than gold enough for both father and son.

III

Glaucus nominated himself to be the presiding Great Senior at the up and coming Great Convocation, winning the vote with very little competition. He had the largest shell among the Golden Ones at that time. Its hue was the brightest because he assiduously polished everyday since childhood. "With a shell like that," his parent's said, "you can go anywhere! You can do anything!" The shell was indeed an asset, perhaps his only one; its radiance led him to imagine he had many others. Early on in school, his only strength was his vanity. In sports, he was a good player to keep on the bench, as just just seeing his bulk threatened opposing teams. Image alone was everything and he gave it his all. When playing "roll-stone," a sort of trilobite soccer, he would dart around the field, abruptly stopping to buff his legs and pick dirt from his claws while teammates ran around in disarray, opponents seizing the advantage. If Glaucus only saw himself, how could be blamed for not seeing others?

His pitch for the Great Senior title was based solely on that he was so large, and the most Golden Trilobite of all. There really hadn't been a Great Senior anything like the first one for thousands of years. That function had become merely ceremonial. Most trilobites loathed being elected to the office, wanting to avoid its many tedious duties: making sure there was ample food, cleaning up the amphitheater, working out seating arrangements, and collecting old shells to be discarded. Since the completion of the Golden Road, excess shells littered the community; getting rid of them would take days beyond the end of the convocation, and the Great Senior of that year would often awake in the morning finding a pile of shells dumped in front of his dwelling.

Custom had also staled the convocation. "Being golden" no longer possessed the aura it once had. The decline of this sentiment accelerated in the following way. Several clever trilobites from the Speckled Tribe discovered how to apply a sheen to their shells, making them pass for Golden. Yellow clay, if smeared and left on shells that had been scratched by sand, would leave a golden patina when gently washed off. These impostors would insinuate themselves among the Goldens at the Great Convocation and enjoy certain privileges reserved for that tribe: extra food, and a chance to mate with one or more of trilobite maidens selected for their physical charms.

This ruse carried on for several decades worth of convocations, the number of impostors increasing with each year, until a speckled trilobite, who overlooked tainting the underside border of his shell, exposed himself at the very moment his shell rolled off during the molting, provoking a scream from his intended partner, who scurried away into the protective fore claws of the Golden harem. The scandal provoked vindictive anger among the Golden Ones, who wanted to ban the Speckled Tribe, or any who conspired with them, from ever attending the convocation at all. A more measured opinion, the one that eventually prevailed, argued that the method of tainting should be admired in itself, a technological advance equal to that of the trilogram.

It was further decided by the mass of Golden Ones, that perhaps the color of gold should not be privileged, that all colors were equal, and that each tribe had the right to hold their own convocation. This, the Golden Ones felt, would maintain the peace. The size of the Great Convocation, led by the Goldens, greatly decreased in number and in prominence. While it was true that color signified no inward merit, that in this respect "fool's gold" and the authentic were the same, there sprung up coteries among the Golden Ones who claimed that perhaps inward merit too was suspect, in a way non-existent, and that in turn, this non-existence haunted all achievements of the Golden Ones, even the great road that led to them. This depreciation of color threatened all trilobites who had little but color to cling to, or thought color the only source of all they wanted to cling to.

None more so than Glaucus, for this change came about just as he was reaching adolescence; growing large, becoming more self-conscious and self-glorious about his appearance—his shell then instantly oxidized by a climate change of opinion! "Great Senior" Glaucus thought he could make the Great Convocation "great" again, an emblem of pride among the Golden Ones. He could have done this by spreading rumors about the Speckled Ones, who started the controversy about color, but chose a safer group to attack—the Pygmies. They were so far away, if indeed they existed at all, that they were not likely to attack; if they did, they would be easily vanquished because so small.

Glaucus went about claiming that the devaluation of gold came about because of Pygmy envy, that the Pygmies had originally discovered the art of tainting, passing it on to the Speckled Ones, who would take the blame. The Pygmies were massing up on the Golden Road, preparing to march in and take all their territories. It was time for the lax and soft to get in shape, and the best exercise was to buff your golden shell every day, buff your own shell, your children's, your wife's, your husband's, your neighbor's. Do it the next day, and every day after that.

On the morning of the Great Convocation, Glaucus the refulgent found himself facing an eager and equally refulgent throng. "Look at us," he said. "Did you ever see anything like us, huh? Did you ever? Now I don't have to tell you about the Pygmies (laughter) and what color they are (laughter)! But I do wanna say this and let me say one thing: *You can call a Pygmy "gold" but you can't make them shine.*" The crowd roared its approval, and repeated the slogan over and over again. This replaced the hallowed "Hail, friend, 'tis a trilobite world!"—a mantra outworn, lacking bite, unsuited for Golden Ones become "great" again.

When Glaucus left the amphitheater, one of his guards noticed a trilogram in tiny stones at the foot of the podium:

Easily bluffed are those completely buffed.

"Left by a malcontent! A Pygmy sympathizer, no doubt," grunted the guard to himself, lifting several legs to kick the stones lest Glaucus come back and see them. But then he paused and set his feet down. "Why bother? After all, *Glaucus can't read.*" The guard felt a slight chill cross his forehead, and shrugged it off. He looked forward to the molting and especially the mating, which he was sure would warm him up.

Fake news!

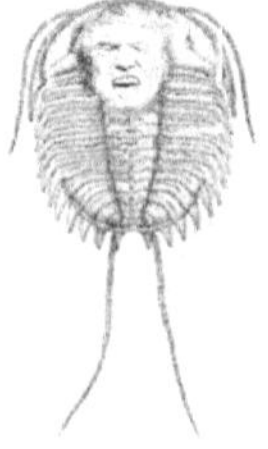

IV

The next day scavenger fish feasted on the remains of the Golden Tribe; the large carcass of Glaucus attracted quite a crowd, mostly the young who mistook quantity for quality. Older scavengers who had followed the trilobite die-off would take their time sorting and picking, while their juniors scarfed without a cultivated, or even nascent sense of connoisseurship. One elder said to another, "Look at them chow down on that tasteless bulk! Did we do that when we were young?"

"Size means nothing, and gold shells even less," the other remarked. "Remember the piquant and succulent flesh we found among the mottled trilobites a couple of days ago? And we had the patience to scout around in order to find it."

The scavengers gorged on trilobite remains for almost a month. Cool waters had stalled the decay of flesh, prolonging the feeding. In scavenger fish lore, this period would be remembered as "The Great Banquet." Younger offspring for several generations hence would hear tales of the many tastes of the many trilobite fillets. Lore of the banquet continued until it grew too old to be believed. "We know it can't have been that wonderful," said a skeptical scavenger descendant. "After all, I am sure then as now, there were many other dishes in the sea."

V

Because Pygmy trilobites were the last to perish, they were the first to figure out the calamity befalling their kind. Lully, their own "Great Senior," (although he abjured the title) and his colleagues had ample time to study the disaster with no way, to be sure, of overcoming it entirely. The seabed of the Pygmies was coarse and dotted with submarine volcanic vents from which lava would spill, steaming turbulence releasing heat to the surrounding waters. As the sea cooled, Lully had his tribe gather around the vents, sending out only the hardy to harvest seaweed for the dwindling community. Many began to weaken. Some others would even venture off into the cold alone, to shorten the wait for what was inevitable. Those that chose that route had a special vent to gather around, where this motto was crudely etched in pumice: "Do not let the darkness lead thee, but lead thyself into the darkness."

Lully and his advisers noted the progress of symptoms as a trilobite succumbed to the cold: a headache first, then sharp pains throughout the limbs and all joints. After a piercing contraction of the chest, often followed by a cry, the trilobite perished, crumpled on the sea floor. All of this would occur within minutes.

Lully crouched by a vent, mesmerized by the boiling; he did the same as a young adult. Back then he was working on what he thought would be a basic chemistry for the trilobite species, something that not even the Golden Ones, with their knack for invention, had considered. Lully surmised that while water was a foundational element of the cosmos, fire was certainly another. Fire and water mixed together, as in the vent, created quite a stir. Then there were the elements of earth, and of air. Perhaps all four combined in a variety of ways and degrees that gave rise to all material forms, living or no. "But of what use are such theories now?" Lully asked himself. Another species in the distant future would make this hypothesis their own and toy around with it for hundreds of years.

His closest comrades and their families had slipped off early in the morning to forage for what seaweed they could find. It was now approaching dusk and none had returned. Lully thought maybe they had planned their exit secretly, too ashamed or too sorrowful to tell him the truth. But thinking wearied him. The vents released a gas in the water, not unlike the vapors that would later rise in the cave of the Delphic Oracle, enhancing her prophetic powers. Lully had lain beside the vent for so long that he dropped into a sleep, spawning many dreams and phantasms. In the last he saw animals not yet born or evolved in his time: a gray hawk perched on a poplar tree, woolly mammoth herds with trunks thrashing about tall grasses, a giant elk drinking from a stream, finally a little human boy squatting in a fire-lit cave, first pressing a palm into ashes, then leaving its imprint, a phantasm of his own, on the cave wall. He crouched next to his father, who dipped his fingers in a clay bowl holding a rich, black sediment. The rough wall of the cave became a field for a huge bison, an image emerging from a fusion of the bison's soul with the father's.

A current of cold water passed over his back side, waking Lully up. He looked around. Beyond the noise of the vent, there was only silence. “Is this the way the world ends, not with a blanket, but a shiver?” he queried aloud. He recalled the little boy in his dream. He yearned to be that strange creature who viewed a meadow unfolding across a torch-lit cave wall. The last trilobite stretched himself into the cauldron. It flared brightly for a moment.

* * *

LIMBO

The Anthropocene Present

We still were on the border of the sea
Like people who are thinking of their road,
Who go in heart and with the body stay.
Dante

This morning Rose delighted in being alone, cradled in the air conditioned comfort of the family SUV, basking in the soft light of her tablet which she had just flicked on. Once her parents settled the bill for their seaside cottage, it was then destination home. Yesterday, vacation's end already so close, was hardly close enough for Rose. She had forgotten to take a sweater or a jacket on the sailboat ride, and the sun burned her shoulders. Disembarking from the boat, she had broken a strap on her sandal; minutes later in the waning evening light, her bare right foot squished the entrails of of a small but very dead and very ripe fish that had washed up at high tide. Now with clean feet in sneakers, her torso sporting a white tank top, shoulders nursed and gleaming with a soothing ointment, she looked forward to her last year of middle school as eagerly as she looked forward to the advent of summer back in May. The sun, the waves, and the fauna, dead or alive, she left to her younger brother, Tommy, who had dashed out of the car to snatch a few last minutes at the beach. Tommy was the darling, perhaps even the offspring of the Elements, whom he had seemingly charmed with his wide-eyed innocence and curiosity. They had not tired of him, and for two weeks he frolicked, unburnt but tanned, hair bleached—indefatigable. On the first day at the beach, Rose had taught him to gather sand and water into hands held together as if in prayer, with fingers pointing towards the earth, funneling a cascade of dull, liquid drops that instantly congealed brightly in the sunlight, festooning the towers and ramparts of a sand castle. He was probably building another now. Rose looked at him through a side window of the SUV, his head bobbing above the ridge that dropped down to the beach; she then then turned to the portal of cyberspace.

"How do you like this '*shell-fie*?'" Rose quickly typed the caption for a photo she had taken of herself earlier in the week. She had found a conch; in the photo she held it covering her nose and cheeks, eyes skewed, mouth in a goofy grin. The caption came to her at breakfast this morning, greatly reviving her spirits after the several mishaps of the sailboat ride and all that followed. The word-play was simple but clever, and accurately punctuated as always. Her closest classmates would have recognized Rose from her writing without the photo or a name. Well immersed and versed in social media, sensitive to its eddies and currents, Rose waited only moments for digital giggles, emoticons and acronyms to sprout on screen. Assured that she was not forgotten, certain that some sort of "welcome back" gathering was most probably already in the works, she closed her tablet and stared out the window. A bumble bee hovered outside the car window, went from left to right and then buzzed off. Tommy jumped up the ridge waving his hands excitedly. Rose opened the door, pausing slightly, stunned by the heat filling the vehicle, and ran towards him. "What's wrong Tommy, are you hurt?"

Tommy shook his head "No." He held up something he just picked up in the shallows:

He looked at her, "Candy?"

Rose smiled at him. "Wow, Tommy! This is a trilobite!"

He tried the new word "tri'bite" then paused for a bit, returning to "Candy?"

"*Candy*? No." Where did he get that idea? Oh, the candy that appeared on store shelves after *Trill b*ecame a hit! Tommy was too young to watch or understand, but he was crazy about the chocolate shells enclosing caramel nougat. The DVD of *Trill* was routine entertainment at sleepovers for more than a year. Favorite scenes were played repeatedly, especially the one in which Trill sang her song. Rose and two of her friends made up a trio whose rendition was a highlight at a class talent show. This past winter, Rose had cracked the DVD, stepping on it when cleaning up her room. It had become already scratched and smudged. She came home one day in spring to find a used but still usable copy laying on her desk. Her mother, thoughtful, and well, motherly, had picked it up at local garage sale. But the Trill *zeitgeist* was over. *Trill 2* was a box office and critical dud. Rose and her friends now were into a television series about teen-age vampires. The boy actors were cute, which helped Rose and company overlook the salient defect of character upon which the whole series turned. Rose observed that vampires would have a easier time nourishing themselves if they lived in a climate zone of long winter nights and short daylight hours. This prompted delayed giggling from the slower wits in Rose's coterie. She was beyond going back to *Trill*, but seeing the film would be a new experience for Tommy.

A car horn blasted. Rose turned to see her parents waving for them to come. "Tommy, there's a movie you can watch at home, and we can get more pictures from the net and I know I still have a small bag of caramel Trilo-treats somewhere in a drawer. (She was relieved later to find this a lucky guess.) Let the stone go. You already have a bucket full of shells. Mom wanted me to dump them on the beach after breakfast, but I saved them for you."

Tommy glanced down at his palm. Once densely moist, the image had turned desiccate and frail.

They heard the car horn blast again. Rose let go of his hand and started to run back up the sandy ridge. Tommy threw the fossil as far as he could out into the water and followed her.

The sea which sometimes yielded its trove to the grasp of human hands, concealed the stone once more.

Made in the USA
Monee, IL
05 September 2020

40808752R00052